THE DAY
THE
ANIMALS
CAME

A Story of
Saint Francis
Day

*To peace and understanding among
the sharers of the earth.*
—F.W.W.

*For my sons, Griffith and Graham Long,
with love from Dad.*
—L.L.

THE DAY THE ANIMALS CAME

A STORY OF SAINT FRANCIS DAY

by FRANCES WARD WELLER

illustrated by LOREN LONG

PHILOMEL BOOKS

IT WAS A GOOD DREAM. RIA WAS running in and out of turquoise water, with raggedy Chico barking at her heels, her lizard in her pocket, and yellow birds calling in the trees along the sand. In the dream she was home.

But the voice that woke her belonged to the crowded room she slept in on this strange new island, where only rats and dusty pigeons roamed free and there wasn't enough sky. They'd come to this New York for a better life, Mami and Papi said back in the stifling summer. But still in October Mami and Papi were always working, working, while Ria stayed with Mrs. Blum, their neighbor, or fidgeted through stuffy days at school.

"Ria Francesca, my *bubeleh*!" It was Mrs. Blum, of course, doing a dance step beside the bed. Mrs. B could make her smile, but she couldn't stretch the sky or put warm Chico back beside her or dim the city lights that hid the stars.

"Time to get up for an adventure!"
Mrs. B waved away Ria's sleepy ques-
tions. "A big surprise, my animal *maven*!
You're going to love it! Trust me!"

So before Ria was really awake they
were trudging along city streets, chew-
ing pretzels from Mr. Clemente's
wagon, with grumpy old Tiger on a
cushion tucked in Mrs. B's grocery cart.
How could they have a proper adventure with Tiger, who hissed at everyone
but Mrs. B? "Why is Tiger coming?" Ria
asked, but Mrs. B shook her head.
"Soon enough you'll see."

They left Mr. Kim's fruit stand and
Perezes' bodega far behind. Things
here looked strange and new. Across
the avenue loomed a church, tall as a
castle in a storybook. "What did I tell
you?" Mrs. B pointed. "There's your
adventure! The cathedral! With all the
animals you could hope to see!"

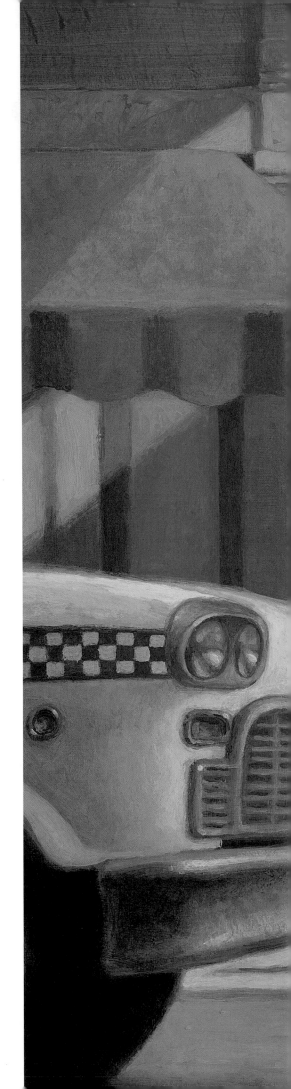

Ria saw banners, balloons, and barricades. And by the time they were halfway across the street, she was tugging Mrs. B along behind her. "Was I right?" Mrs. B waved her arms. "Is this terrific? It's the—whaddya call it—feast, of your name saint, Francis! Was he a *mensch*, a truly noble person!"

A pair of huge black dogs sat drooling on the cathedral's driveway, and behind them the line of animals with their people stretched way around the block. Mrs. B beamed at Ria. "Because Saint Francis loved the animals, we'll go in soon and all these will be blessed! Even Tiger!" cried Mrs. B. "Even an elephant!"

Oh, Ria knew about her good Saint Francis. He called the sun and moon and animals his brothers and sisters. "Hello, Brother Wolf," he'd say. "Hello, Sister Pig!" But as Mrs. B bubbled on, just one thing mattered to Ria. She was the only one without an animal for blessing.

Then something furry brushed her ankles and a raggedy dog streaked away, trailing a leash. Without a thought Ria ran after him.

Up the driveway, in and out of a garden, past dancers and jugglers, up rough stairs, and through an open door.

Only when she'd pounced upon the leash and gathered in the pup did she realize she was inside the cathedral. Fat stone pillars stood around her like giant tree trunks, hung with flowers, touched with light.

"He's mine!" cried a voice behind her, and another hand grabbed the leash. "He got away when we left the taxi! Thanks for catching him!" For a moment she'd thought she had an animal for blessing. But the dog and his boy were gone.

Ria stood in a river of pets and people. Everywhere she turned was someone too tall to see around. Where had she come in, and how could she find Mrs. B? Not only now was she without an animal. She was alone besides.

Jostled by the crowd, she bumped into something solid. A statue. Ria gazed up at a bronze wolf, all rumpled, with his head thrown back to howl. Something fluttered in her stomach. That wolf looked far from home too. But maybe from that wolf's back she could see Mrs. B.

She pulled herself up, clamped her hands on the wolf's back, and caught her breath. A tall, important-looking lady with a long robe and a walkie-talkie was staring at her.

"What do you think you're doing?" the lady demanded.

Ria clung to the wolf. Her eyes stung. She couldn't find Mrs. B and now she was in trouble too. She could only shake her head.

But Mrs. B burst round a pillar, carrying Tiger like a football. "She's lost!" puffed Mrs. B. "She's new here! Homesick! Missing pets she left behind!"

Ria slid slowly down and rubbed her eyes. She found Mrs. B and the tall lady nodding at each other. "Come on," the lady said to Ria. "My name is Mary. I've something you might like to see."

They followed her across the church's nave and into sunlight.

Outside, a weedy field stretched to city streets. But Ria hardly saw it. For scattered here and clustered there, still coming out of trucks and vans, were—oh!—amazing animals. A dog as big as a pony. A horse as small as the dog. A bird that might be an eagle.

"Wait here a minute," Mary said. But Mrs. B was busy calming Tiger, and beyond the woman with a macaw on each shoulder were steps. At the foot of the steps were tethered a shaggy cow and a goat.

Ria crept down. Something rustled and sputtered in the cage beside the cow. It was a duck, huddled in the back corner. Maybe she could soothe it like the sugar birds who used to share her breakfast. *"¡Hola, pato!"* Ria unlatched the cage's door. But the duck erupted from the cage and flapped away.

Ria ran after him. That duck just wanted to be someplace else, but he was headed for city traffic. Ria could hear Mrs. B calling and clucking behind her, but she had to catch that duck! So down the field they scrambled, past a haughty owl, through knots of photographers, and under llamas, till the duck landed with a happy plop in a big puddle behind a barricade and beside an elephant.

"Hey," laughed the handler washing down the elephant's back, "is your duck tryin' ta spook my Cora?"

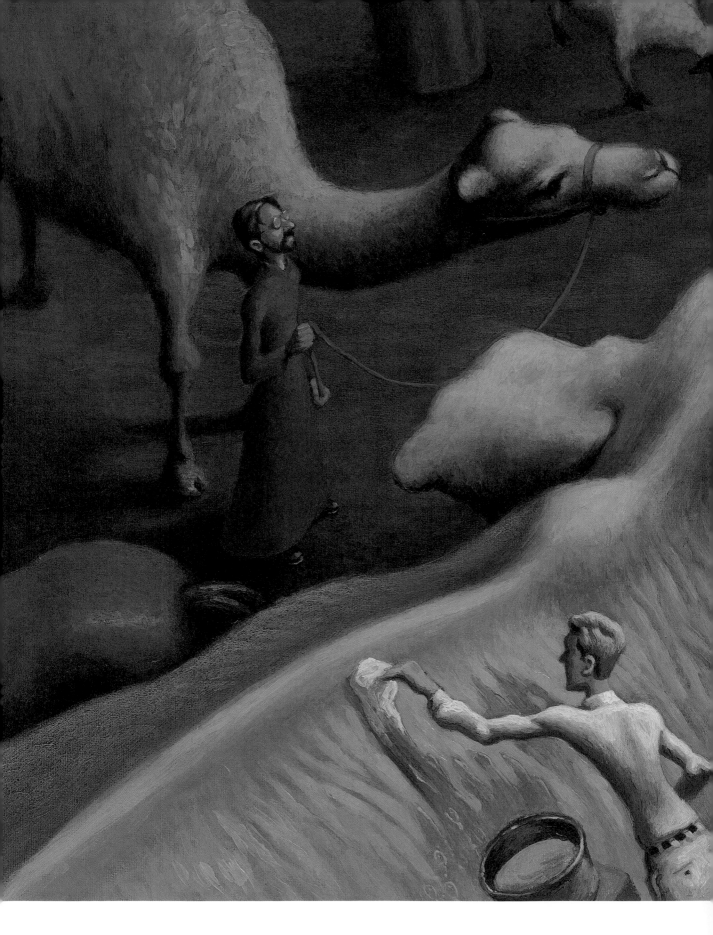

Ria sighed as she plunked herself down in the weeds. "Not my duck." And how could she catch him? She reached into her pocket. The duck stopped splashing. As Ria pulled out her last crumbs of pretzel, the

duck stretched out his neck and waddled closer. He was eating from her lap when Mary laughed behind them. "You've charmed our Groucho!" Mary cried. "You're just the one to take him in for blessing!"

Ria's heart thumped. She wanted to see what was going to happen in the cathedral—oh, she did! But it would be scary to be in charge of the pesky duck.

"This little guy can surely use a blessing," Mary went on cheerily as she pinned Ria into the smallest robe remaining. "Just bravely march him to the bishop. And smile! We're celebrating all Creation!" She put the flustered duck in Ria's arms and set her in the long line following Cora and a cranky camel to the cathedral's front doors.

In the crowd's hush every shuffling foot and paw seemed noisy. So did Groucho's mumbling, and the quacks he blurted at every echoey bark and whistle. But Ria marched on. No matter what, she must get him to that altar for his blessing.

Faces watched from everywhere, dark and light and every shade between. A beautiful old lady, smiling, tears running in the wrinkles on her cheeks. A giant black man cradling a white mouse. Two littler girls who gazed at her in wonder.

Groucho lurched and nipped at Ria's sleeve. She strained sideways to see how far they had to go. The falcon just ahead threw out its wings and sprang up on its tether, and Groucho tried to dive under her arm. Ria gripped him tight and hardly breathed. "Stay with me, Brother Duck!" she whispered. "We're nearly there!"

Groucho grumbled and muttered and wriggled. Ria held him as tightly as she dared. Halfway up the long cascade of steps the camel balked and bellowed, and the duck quacked madly in reply. "No, no! *¡Silencio!*" Ria murmured as she climbed higher.

Then Cora disappeared between the towering bronze doors. The camel and the man with the falcon riding on his glove were moving too. The church beyond yawned like a cavern. Lined with breathing walls of pets and people, the aisle they walked stretched to a far-off altar.

Ria took a big breath and stepped through the doors. This was a holy day, due great respect. She was part of it now. Like a raft on a river, she could only keep going.

For Cora stopped, and then she turned to start a circle round the altar. The camel turned, and then the falcon handler. So Ria stood before the bishop after all! The man with the golden staff smiled and raised his free hand above Ria's duck. "Rejoice in all God's creatures," he murmured for only her to hear.

Tucked between Cora and a man wrapped in a python, Ria stroked the duck's back and watched the circle grow around the altar. "Go in peace," the bishop finally said. Instead the duck squirmed as the crowd boomed into a last song. Cora fidgeted too, tossing her head and shuffling her feet. But below the singing Ria heard the elephant handler's steady voice: "Cora—dance! Dance! Dance!" And suddenly Cora plodded from side to side, swinging her great head with the rhythm of the hymn. "For the beauty of the earth, sing, oh, sing today."

The elephant danced. And then the man with the python danced as well. Mrs. B swayed with a drowsy Tiger, and Mary two-stepped with her walkie-talkie. And all at once Ria was dancing too, with Groucho quiet in her arms and her face raised to the vault above, so high it seemed another sort of sky.

Around her, voices rang like thunder, and the great dome of the cathedral seemed to shelter the whole family of Earth. So maybe she belonged here after all. For if all creatures were her family, then maybe all the world was home.

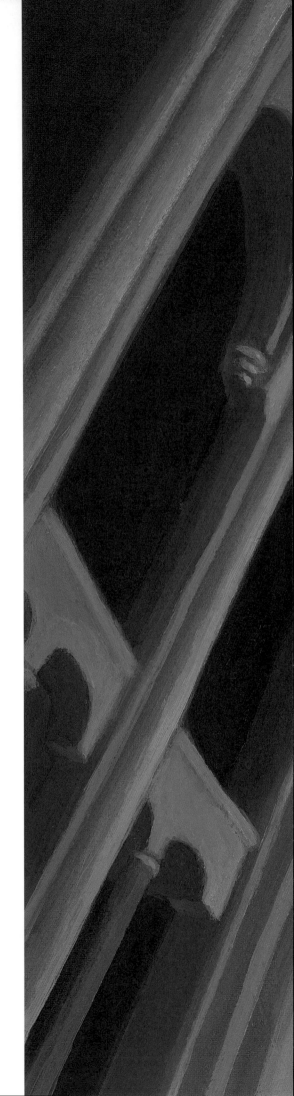

AUTHOR'S NOTE

Saint John the Divine, the world's largest Gothic cathedral, stands on the Upper West Side of Manhattan Island in New York City, near Central Park, Harlem, Columbia University, Jewish delis, and Latino bodegas. The great church is a hardworking servant of its diverse neighborhood—a haven of food, shelter, counseling, and a home for the creative arts. It is also a vital center for traditional worship, and often the city's chosen place for celebration, mourning, or reconciliation.

People flock there from near and far for special celebrations of summer and winter solstices, a Native American Thanksgiving, and a New Year's Eve ceremony of peace. But the Feast of Saint Francis, celebrated on the first Sunday in October, draws the biggest gathering of all to the Episcopal cathedral. Some three thousand people of all creeds and colors—and countless animals—come to celebrate the wonders of nature and the interdependence of all life on Earth in a joyful outpouring of prayer, dance, and the music of Paul Winter's *Missa Gaia* (Mass for the Earth).

Blessing the animals is a fitting way to celebrate the feast of Saint Francis of Assisi. Seven hundred years ago, Francis preached that all creatures must live in harmony, respecting the earth and one another, and his life was a lesson in what he preached. So now, all these centuries later, he is thought of not only as the patron saint of animals but of ecology as well. It's said Saint Francis so loved and revered nature that even as he lay dying he wrote the *Canticle of Brother Sun*, which inspired the opening hymn of the *Missa Gaia*.

ACKNOWLEDGMENTS

Thanks to all who told me their own stories of Saint Francis' feast
day: Richard Brown; Alta, Clark, and Jeremiah Buden; the Reverend Joel
Gibson; Pati Mayfield; Peggy Munves; Vince Sharp;
Lore Schirokauer; Andrea Yost; and especially Mary Bloom,
longtime conjurer and soul of the procession that celebrates Creation,
whose generous help truly made this book possible.
Thanks too to Lucy and Luis Perez, Trisha Perez Kennealy,
Dr. Eugene Saklad, Mim Selig, and Alissa Stayn, who advised on
Hebrew, Spanish, and Yiddish.
Special thanks to Wayne Kempton, archivist of the Episcopal
Diocese of New York, for his assistance in providing
reference photographs and background information.

Saint John the Divine is the largest cathedral in the world. Its construction
began in 1897; however, the towers have never been completed. In this book, artist
Loren Long envisioned a finished cathedral, a promise of the cathedral to come. He
also took artistic liberties with the scene of the blessing, creating art that enhances
the animals' circle (which would actually be crowded with people around an altar)
while remaining true to the spirit of the event.

You can learn more about the cathedral and its history at
www.stjohndivine.org.

PATRICIA LEE GAUCH, EDITOR

Designed by Semadar Megged.
Text set in 15.5-point Golden Cockerel.
The illustrations are rendered in acrylic on canvas.

Library of Congress Cataloging-in-Publication Data
Weller, Frances Ward.
The day the animals came: a story of Saint Francis Day / by Frances Ward Weller ;
illustrated by Loren Long. p. cm.
Summary: A young girl who misses her former home and her animal friends left behind
in the West Indies makes new friends at the blessing of the animals at a cathedral
in New York City on the Feast of St. Francis.
[1. Neighbors—Fiction. 2. Animals—Fiction. 3. Hispanic Americans—Fiction.
4. New York (N.Y.)—Fiction.] I. Long, Loren, ill. II. Title. PZ7.W454 Day 2003
[E]—dc21 2002006297

ISBN 0-399-23630-9
1 3 5 7 9 10 8 6 4 2
First Impression